AF491746

A Gun and a Collar for Saragosa

C RAIG A RROYO

Copyright © 2024 Craig Arroyo
All rights reserved
First Edition

NEWMAN SPRINGS PUBLISHING
320 Broad Street
Red Bank, NJ 07701

First originally published by Newman Springs Publishing 2024

ISBN 979-8-89308-590-7 (Paperback)
ISBN 979-8-89308-591-4 (Digital)

Printed in the United States of America

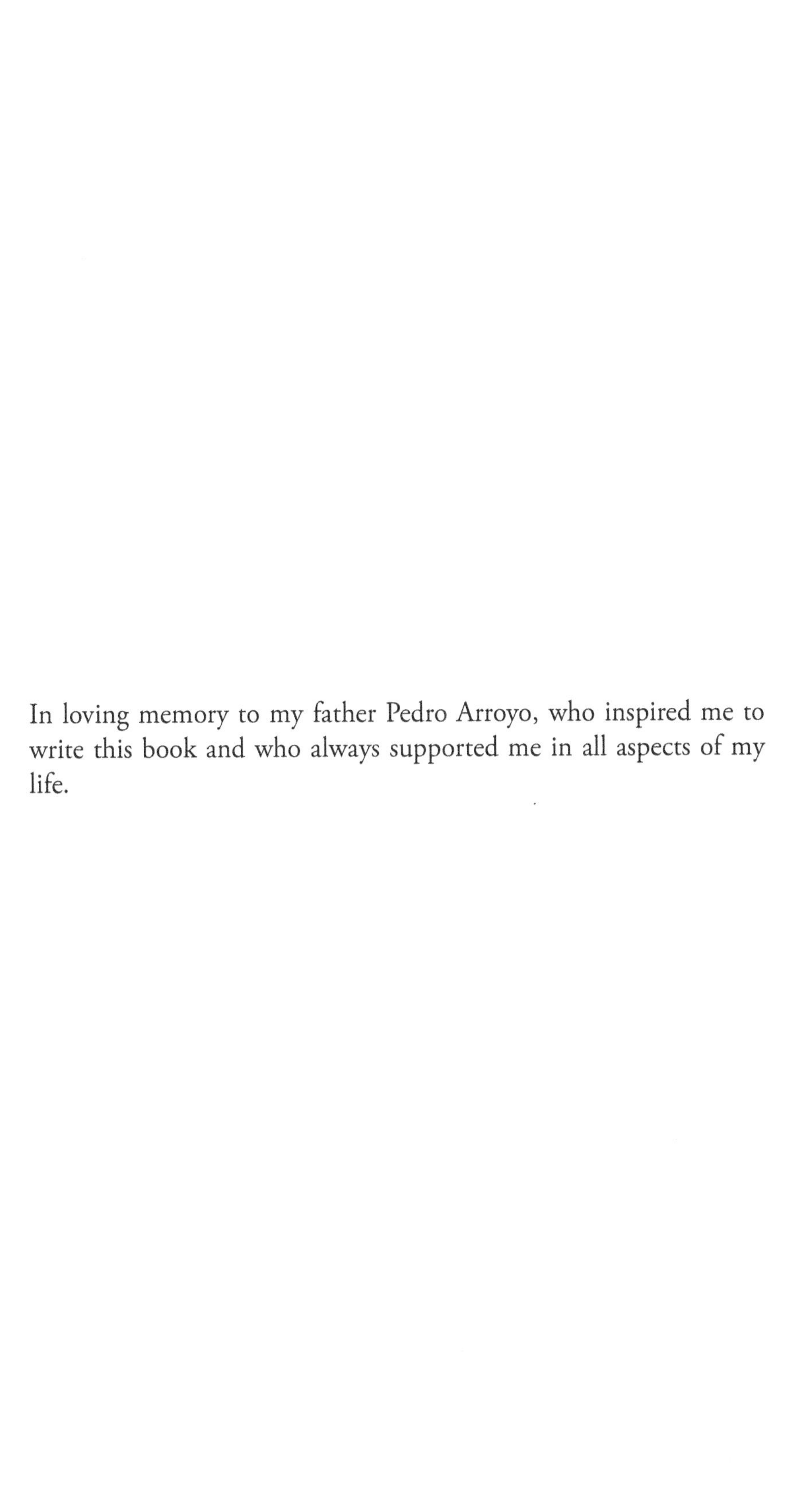

In loving memory to my father Pedro Arroyo, who inspired me to write this book and who always supported me in all aspects of my life.

The year was 1865. A year of sleepless nights and bad dreams. See, that year, I was a member of the US Army fighting a war known to everyone as the Civil War. As one of the US Army's top Yankee soldiers, I was called upon to see a lot of action on the front line, but I felt something in my soul that I had never felt before: fear. Fear that the end was near. How many more times could I go out in the line of fire and come out alive?

When all looked negative, I always found positivity in my squad leader, Captain Tuckett. Captain Tuckett was the kind of guy who was never on the downside. He always carried a small box around, and many of the soldiers always wondered what was in there. He would just respond, "It's my Bible to drive away evil spirits." On the front line one night, things were really beginning to go bad, and again I began to feel that fear of dying. When it was all over, I began to read a Bible that a soldier once gave me. I guess with the fear that I had that the end was near, I thought it would be a good time to try and get on the Lord's good side.

Every time Captain Tuckett saw me reading the Bible, he would tell me, "In this box, I have what will drive away evil spirits forever." The word had come down from the higher-ups that the US Army was losing too many soldiers and that something had to be done fast. The one thing the US Army always had over the Confederate Army were lion guts to lay it all on the line and charge." To make a statement against the rebels on the other side of the war, we all decided to go along with the plan and charge.

The night before the charge was the worst night of them all. This was the night that I was positive would be my last night on earth. That night, Captain Tuckett and I were going over old war stories when he took a look at my Bible and said that I had earned the right to see his Bible that drove away evil spirits. In the box, he pulled out the most beautiful six-shooter I had ever seen—silver chrome with a white pearl handle. The six-shooter was given to him by his father before he died, and he always carried it for good luck, not for action. I must admit, up until that night, the six-shooter was a bit of good luck.

At the end of the night, I decided to do what I thought I would never do. I decided to make a deal with God. With my Bible in hand, I got on my knees and prayed. I told God I had a real bad feeling about the upcoming charge and that if I made it out alive, I would dedicate my life to him. As the sun slowly began to crack, I could hear a loud voice yell, "ATTENTION! COME ON, PINECONE, GET UP." Captain Tuckett always called me Pinecone because he could never pronounce my last name. Before the charge, Captain Tuckett gave us all a pep talk, and he personally came up to me and told me, "Pinecone, if something happens to me, I want you to remember that my Bible will drive away evil spirits quicker than your Bible."

As we looked across the field at the Confederate Army, I couldn't stop thinking about death, which made my deal with God that much stronger. Slowly, we grabbed our guns, and I could hear absolutely nothing but the loud yell of Captain Tuckett, "CHARGE!

With guns blazing, we all attacked. As I ran, shooting my guns, I could hear the gunfire and the bodies dropping one by one. Somehow, Captain Tuckett and I wound up side by side, and one by one, we were dropping rebs. All of a sudden, I heard a loud yell, and I saw a tall rebel in front of me knocking my guns out of my hands with a hickory stick. It appeared that during the action, he had lost his guns. As a result of all the gun smoke in the air, I couldn't see what he looked like, but I could read his name on his uniform: Riley. This was the soldier we had heard about who almost got a dishonorable discharge for torturing some of his own men.

As we engaged in hand-to-hand combat, Captain Tuckett went on to handle some of the other rebel soldiers. With kicks and punches flying, Riley and I were pretty much evenly matched until slowly, I began to get the upper hand. As we made our way toward each other, it began to rain, and small puddles of mud began to build up everywhere, making it hard to keep our balance. As Riley fought to get back on his feet, he found a gun from a nearly dead soldier. Riley pointed the gun at me, and I was so in shock that I could not move. My destiny that I spoke to God about was near.

Suddenly, out of nowhere, I heard a familiar yell, "No!" It was Captain Tuckett, jumping in front of the bullet. Before Riley could get another shot off, I was gone in the rain and wound up behind him. Knocking his gun out of his hand, I proceeded to pound, punch, and kick Riley with no mercy. This son of a bitch just shot my best friend, and he was going to pay. As I beat him within an inch of his life, I could hear Captain Tuckett mutter, "Pinecone." Riley was down and nearly beaten to death, so I made my way toward Captain Tuckett. As his dying eyes looked at me, his last words were, "Take my gun and holster for yourself, and always remember, this right here is what really drives away the evil spirits."

As I closed Captain Tuckett's eyes, out of nowhere, Riley jumped on me again with what little strength he had left. As I wrestled him off me, I grabbed him by his greasy, wet black hair and proceeded to dunk his head in a nearby mud puddle. Somehow, desperately kicking and gasping for air, he managed to get his hand on the same gun again, reached back, and—*BANG!*—shot me in the right eye. That was the last thing I could remember about my last day in the Civil War.

*****

When I woke up, what felt like a ten-minute nap was actually a two-week semicoma. Everything was fuzzy, and when I made my way off the bed, I realized I had a black patch over my right eye. At that moment, it all came back to me: the Civil War, that bastard Riley, the gunshot to my right eye, and Captain Tuckett. My squad leader and best friend, gone. What hurt the most was that that no-good son of a bitch Riley was still alive, from what I recalled. As I removed the patch to see what my battle scar looked like, I heard a young lady's voice say, "Don't do that. You could get your eye infected. Now get back in bed and relax, Mr. Pinekin."

"Where am I?" I asked her.

She replied, "You're in La Hospital de Dios in Texas."

All I could think about was what a crazy world we live in. One minute, you're fighting a meaningless war in North Carolina; the next, you're all bandaged up in Texas. I asked her what her name was and how she knew mine. She told me her name was Carmen and that I was sent here by the US Army with my belongings: a gold medal of honor, $100,000 cash provided by the US Army for being named a war hero, and one beautiful white paper that said "Honorable Discharge for Wounded in Action Veteran." Beside my right eye being blown off and Captain Tuckett's death, all this was like a blessing. "A blessing from God!"

At that point, I also remembered the deal I made with God: if I lived, I would dedicate my life to him." Two months later, I was released from the hospital, and Carmen asked me what I intended on doing. I responded, "I'm going to saddle up my horse and slowly but surely make my way toward Mexico."

"Why Mexico, Mr. Pinekin?" she asked.

"To do the work of the Lord," I replied.

As Carmen handed me my belongings, the last thing she handed me was Captain Tuckett's box with the chrome six-shooter and holster. Carmen asked, if I was going to Mexico to do the work of the Lord, why I was carrying a six-shooter. I told her the story of Captain Tuckett, and she told me that for the right reason, she would return to her home country. That's when I asked her to be my personal nurse for the mission I was building. She responded, "Mission, Mr. Pinekin?"

"Yes, a mission, with my own priests' convent, school, and church. From this day forward, I shall be known as Father Pinekin, and my Savior and dedication would be the Lord God and Jesus Christ."

Carmen smiled, and we both saddled our horses and off we rode to our destiny in Saragosa, Mexico. As we headed to the Mexican border, Carmen asked me why I chose the small town of Saragosa to open the mission. During the two months I lay in the hospital, besides studying to become a priest, I would read newsletters to keep up with current events. One thing that particularly caught my eye was the story I read about the poor children in Mexico—in particular, the very small town of Saragosa, a town so small and so poor that there wasn't even a school. I felt that that was my calling.

As Carmen and I rode through Saragosa, I pulled up to the mayor's office. I gradually explained to him who I was and what my intentions were for his town. At seven o'clock that evening, Carmen and I had supper with Mayor Fernandez. I explained that I was a former soldier in the US Army who was honorably discharged and compensated very well for my time served and that I had moved to Saragosa for a better life for me and for the people in this town.

Mayor Fernandez gave me all rights to the center part of the town where everyone from all over Saragosa could visit. As Carmen cried tears of joy, the townspeople and I went right to work. First thing I noticed was the size of the land. I mean, acres and acres of open beautiful land, and it was all mine. The townspeople first helped me build the school so that the children could start getting an education. Next came the mission, so all the orphans and homeless children of Saragosa could have a place to live, and last came the church. My church, my beautiful church, with twelve rows, a beautiful altar, and a beautiful seven-foot cross at the top of the church. I was so excited that I performed my first sermon that very Sunday. Carmen attended, all of the town's children and parents attended, and at the head of the church was Mayor Fernandez.

As I spoke the word of the Lord and went on and on about how proud I was of such a small town to come together and work with each other to create the wonderful miracle of God, I thanked the mayor, I thanked the kids and parents, and I gave a special thanks to my best friend Carmen, who was now the school's teacher and the mission's nurse. Yes, it was the beginning of something great. For the first time in a long time, I felt positive. I felt like finally, all the suffering I had done in the past had finally paid off.

*****

From my office, I used to have my telegrams delivered. I used to start my mornings off by reading the *American News* newspaper. I always liked to keep up with current events, but mainly I used to keep up with the Civil War news. Five hundred thousand deaths to pray for and counting. Remembering my days in the US Army, I would sometimes see hundreds of soldiers lying dead and feel like that was a lot of dead men. Now as I read my newspaper and read about five hundred thousand deaths, sometimes I couldn't bear but feel like I should be in the war protecting some of those men. My heart bled to hear about so many deaths, but at the same time, I felt that those men were also lucky because now they were in the hands of the Lord.

As I got on my knees to pray for those five hundred thousand souls, I often wondered if, even if the war does end and either the Confederate or US Army won, what actually was won? And I also believed that if either side won, all the men who fought in that war have actually lost. After my morning read of the *American News* newspaper, I would walk over to the school and mission to visit the kids. When I went to the class, many of the kids had a lot of questions about my eye. Carmen and I explained to all the kids about my past experience in the Civil War, and many of the kids thought it was pretty exciting to have a priest who knew a thing or two about action. Seeing those smiling faces and seeing Carmen so happy teaching in the school and nursing the kids in the mission is what kept me at ease.

The next morning, as I made my way to my office, I got to thinking about Captain Tuckett and the gun he gave me before he died. Although I was now a priest who stood against guns, it was my only memento of Captain Tuckett. I took the six-shooter and placed it in a closet next to a statue of Jesus Christ on the cross. As I read my telegrams, I could not stop thinking about Captain Tuckett, so to unwind, I picked up the newspaper, and on the front page was a face that had haunted me for months: Riley. As I stared at that all-too-familiar rugged face, I proceeded to read the article. Riley, a soldier in the Confederate Army, was dishonorably discharged from that army and removed from his duty in the Civil War along with two other

Confederate soldiers, Gordon and Reese, for hanging six colored soldiers who were also a part of the Confederate Army.

Riley, Reese, and Gordon were all sent to a county jail to wait trial for first degree murder. It was bad enough to be fighting a war against men who do not know you and were trying to kill you, but to be killed by men who were supposed to be on your own side was really horrible.

The trial was set for March 1. All of Riley's, Gordon's, and Reese's past sheets were brought in front of the US marshal's desk. It was not long before a hanging date was set. These three Civil War renegade outlaws were getting there just deserts.

*****

"Ladies and gentlemen, on March 1, these three men were tried and convicted for the murder of six innocent colored Confederate soldiers. Riley, Gordon, Reese, do you three men have any last words?"

All three men at the same time responded, "We're brought to this world out of our own will and taken out of this world on our own will!"

As the executioner went to pull the latch, loud yells and gunshot started going off. Out of the sunset, a female riding a horse shot all three knots and the executioner. As the marshal and his men tried to gun the lady down, Riley jumped backward over his tied-up hands, a trick he learned during his days as a soldier. He grabbed a member of the US marshal group and choked him to death, grabbed his guns, and began shooting all the members of the US marshals' group. As Riley was gunning everyone down, the female rider was cutting Gordon's and Reese's ropes off their hands, and handed each one a six-shooter. Bullets were flying everywhere, and finally, Riley crept up behind the US marshal and called to him, "Hey!" As the marshal turned around, Riley shot him between the eyes. The four outlaws rode out in a daring escape. As they rode into the mountains, Riley got off his horse, and so did the girl. Riley looked at her and yelled, "Sissy!" They both kissed and hugged. Apparently, Sissy was Riley's last girlfriend before the Civil War.

"Girl, what took you so long?" Riley asked.

Sissy responded, "I was picking the right time to come for you." It appeared that Sissy read about Riley and the others hanging on the *World News* newspaper and came to their rescue.

"Well," Reese began to talk. "We killed six nigger soldiers, killed a US marshal and five deputies, we're on the run for all these crimes, and by now, we all have to have a bounty on all of our heads. So what do we do for fun next, Riley?"

Riley responded, "Well, guys, I say we rob a couple of banks, rob a couple of trains, and when we're done robbing, we all make our way to Mexico."

"Why Mexico?" Gordon asked.

Riley responded, "'Cause there's plenty of open land out there for the takin'.""

"You know I'm with you wherever you go, baby." Sissy chuckled.

"Yeah, I know." Riley bent over and kissed Sissy. "Let's go."

*****

Back in Saragosa, I was still at peace with myself. I spoke to Carmen about Riley, and I also read to her about their escape. Carmen responded that they were far from us and knew nothing about where we were. She said Riley was a ghost from the past that I should just let go. Sleepless nights wondering about this man's whereabouts, and now he was on the loose with three other outlaws. I knew for some reason deep in my heart that our paths would some-day come together.

The next day at the mission was a really bad day. I began to feel really—I mean *really*—nervous, with sweaty palms; and to top it all, I began to get flashbacks about the Civil War. Then I began to see visions of Riley everywhere I went. The halls, the church, the mission… I kept on seeing him. It got to the point where I would throw my belongings everywhere out of anger. Carmen saw what I was going through and would walk me to my office, wipe my cold-sweated face, and tell me to stop worrying over nothing. I couldn't stop; everything I did, everywhere I went, Riley was there. Every time I looked in the mirror and saw my eye, I couldn't help but remember that day in the Civil War when he blew my eye right out of my face. That day, I went to the chapel and prayed to God to keep Riley and his gang as far away from Mexico as possible. It was not even worth praying for them because I knew no matter what, they were lost souls, and there was nothing that I could do to make them change their lives.

Carmen constantly would console me and would always bring some of the children from the mission to make me feel better. There was one little boy named Pedro who always knew how to make me smile. Although he was Mexican-born and raised, he knew the words of the "Star-Spangled Banner" and would sing them to me. Pedro always knew that hearing that song always made me smile.

Pedro would look at me and say, "Are you okay, Padre?" And I would respond, "I am now, Pedro." Pedro lost both his parents to outlaws who were stealing innocent people's land. Since the age of six, he had been without a home or a family. Now with the mission I built, there was hope for him. Carmen would look at me when Pedro would leave and say, "I know if I brought Pedro over to see you, it would bring a smile to your face." It was very comforting to feel that when you felt down, you had people who cared enough for you to come to your aid.

The next morning, I felt much better: no cold sweats, no sweaty palms, no flashbacks, no nothing. That little talk that Carmen and Pedro gave me really helped. One day, I even threw a little fiesta for everyone just because I was feeling good.

*****

Back in the States, Riley and the Renegade Outlaws—that was the name he gave his posse—were planning their first bank robbery. As they rode their horses to the front of the bank, Sissy, wearing a blue church outfit, would walk up to the teller as if she were making a deposit. As the teller went to take her money, she pulled out a two-shot derringer out of a holster on her leg, and then Riley, Gordon, and Reese all shot once to the air. Riley, who was the ringleader, yelled out to everyone, "Okay, folks, this is a holdup. My boys are going to go around and take all your money and all your expensive belongings. And me, I'm gonna play a numbers game with you." He pointed his six-shooter at the teller.

Riley leaned over to the teller and said, "If I asked you nicely what the combination to that safe was, you'd give it to me, wouldn't you?"

The teller responded, "I don't know the combination."

Riley pointed his gun downward, shot the teller's pinky off, and said, "You want to keep the other nine fingers?"

The teller, in pain, nodded and opened the safe.

As they made their way out of the bank, a crippled Civil War veteran in the bank recognized Riley. "Riley!" the man called.

Riley turned around, saw the man on crutches, and said, "How the hell do you know my name?"

The man responded, "Just a few months ago, we were fighting on the battlefield in the Civil War. I need to warn you. There's a $2,000 bounty on your head."

Riley responded "Two thousand only? Darn, looks like I need to work harder."

As Riley and the Renegades made their way out the door, a US marshal from a nearby town was waiting and began to open fire. Not realizing that Riley now had a posse, the US marshal focused all of his attention on Riley. As bullets blazed between Riley and the marshal, somehow, Gordon, Reese, and Sissy made their way with all the money, cut through the back of the bank, and rode up behind the US marshal.

BANG, BANG, BANG, BANG, BANG, BANG, BANG, BANG, BANG! All three put so many holes in the US marshal that he was drowning in his own blood. As Riley made his way out of the bank, he also opened fire on the already dead US marshal and shot him six more times in cold blood.

As all four were getting ready to ride off, Riley yelled, "I'm Riley, and this here are the Renegade Outlaws. Now, all you kind folks run and tell every US marshal, sheriff, and bounty hunter to stay out of our way, or there will be more bloodshed just like this every time. Heeyah!" Off the Renegade Outlaws rode onto their next destiny.

Riley told the Renegade Outlaws about his bounty and that by now everyone must know about the Renegade Outlaws. They were so excited about their first robbery that they went out and robbed another bank that day. The Renegade Outlaws were making a lot of enemies quickly in a short amount of time.

*****

My *World News* paper came in at eight Monday morning, and there it was, a big picture of all four outlaws. "WANTED DEAD OR ALIVE," $2,000 for the capture of Riley, and another $1,000 for any member of the Renegade Outlaws. I called Carmen over and showed her the picture. She had always heard about Riley from my stories but had never seen an actual photo. As she looked at the paper, the very picture of Riley made her shake.

"Is this the man?" she said nervously. "Is this the man who shot your eye off?"

I couldn't help but feel anger. I looked at Carmen, and as I was getting ready to break down, a beautiful young voice in the air began to sing "The Star-Spangled Banner."

"PEDRO!" I yelled. "WHAT ARE YOU DOING HERE?"

Pedro responded, "I made you a present, Padre."

As he handed me the box, I felt the warm comfort that Pedro always made me feel. When I opened the box, there were four beautiful rosaries.

"Why four?" I asked Pedro.

"Every color has a special meaning. The red one is for when you're angry, the white one is for when you're relaxing, and the blue one is for when you're happy. My favorite one is this one, Padre. It is dark blue and yellow. Those are the colors you wore when you were in the army. The other three rosaries put together are red, white, and blue. The colors of your beautiful flag, Padre."

Since all four rosaries had colors that each signified one mood I was in, I decided to wear all four at the same time because of my mixed emotions. I didn't know how to feel.

The following day, Carmen brought my newspaper, and it appeared that a stagecoach making its way to the Mexican border was robbed, leaving three dead Yankee soldiers.

*****

The bounty on Riley went up from $2,000 to $2,500, and the rest of the posse (Gordon, Reese, and Sissy) were worth fifteen hundred apiece. The strongbox in the stagecoach was filled with US federal gold, and the one who knew about the stagecoach and where it was headed was Sissy.

Sissy, while out on the town, saw a US soldier with two others and knew that if they weren't fighting the war, they were sent out on a special mission. That US federal gold was to make it to Mexico but never did. Sissy got that Yankee to tell her what was in the strongbox, where they were going, what day they were leaving, and at what time. Before you knew it, Sissy went back to Riley, and the following week, before the three US soldiers could even reach the Mexican border, the Renegade Outlaws were waiting for them. Riley and his gang had really outdone themselves and were looking only to get richer. These Renegade Outlaws were not going to stop robbing and murdering until each one made enough money to live happily for the rest of their lives.

*****

The following morning, when I went to visit the kids at the school, I went to show them my new rosary beads that Pedro made for me. I told Carmen when she was done teaching to meet me at my office; I had to discuss something very important with her. After I left, I went straight to my office and stood there basically all day until Carmen arrived.

When Carmen arrived, I told her that I realized something very disturbing. Riley and the Renegade Outlaws had been robbing banks, trains, and stagecoaches all through San Antonio, Dallas, Houston, and the last job they did was robbing the US Army stagecoach in El Paso, just a few hundred miles from the Mexican border. I told Carmen that I felt they were working their way toward Mexico. Carmen saw all the signs also and told me to do what I thought was right. I told Carmen I was going to pray all night that these outlaws got caught. But I was not going to let anyone come to Saragosa and take away my life.

*****

Back in El Paso, Sissy was starting to feel a little on edge about their next job. The word was out now that each member of the Renegade Outlaws was worth an equal $2,500 each—$10,000 for the lucky sheriff, lawman, or bounty hunter who could bring in all four. But we all knew that the task of bringing in all four members of the Renegade Outlaws was a lot easier said than done.

Sissy was getting tired of all the chances they were taking and wanted to speed up crossing the border to start a more civilized life with Riley.

"Gordon," Riley called. "What do you look forward to in Mexico?"

Gordon responded, "I look forward to buying a large acre of land, drinking a lot of tequila, and sleeping with a lot of them greasy Mexican women."

"What about you, Reese?"

"I look forward to relaxing all day and all night. Hey, Riley, what are you looking forward to?"

"I'm looking forward to buying a large chunk of land and settling down with my wife!"

Sissy looked at Riley and yelled, "WHAT THE HELL DO YOU MEAN SETTLING DOWN WITH YOUR WIFE? YOU NEVER TOLD ME YOU HAD A WIFE IN MEXICO, YOU BASTARD!"

Riley grabbed Sissy and said, "I don't, but when we get to Mexico, that will be your job." Sissy looked at Riley, confused, and Riley said, "Sissy, will you be my wife?"

Sissy, with tears in her eyes, screamed, "Yes, baby! Yes! Oh, Riley, I love you!"

Riley responded, "I love you too, girl."

Gordon and Reese pulled out a bottle of whiskey and toasted to the new happy couple.

Gordon told Riley that the Federal Reserve Bank of El Paso was only a couple hundred feet from the Mexican border and that there was going to be a lot of money and gold delivered tomorrow. "The best thing to do is to lie low for a few days, and then we go and make our move."

Riley responded, "We need to act fast. With twenty-five hundred riding on all our heads, every US marshal, every sheriff, and every bounty hunter is looking to put a bullet between each one of our eyes. When we hit the bank, start shooting when we leave. We don't know who's going to be out there waiting for us. Also, as we head for the border, there will be border patrol officers trying to prevent us from crossing. We must also take them out. Once we're in Mexico, we will decide from there what we'll do."

All the others agreed.

*****

Early Friday morning, four horses pulled up to the Federal Reserve Bank of El Paso. Three cold-eyed, rough-looking men and one tiny brunette. It was the Renegade Outlaws. Like clockwork, Sissy went up to the teller as if to make a deposit. As the teller went for the money, Riley stuck his bowie knife right through his hand. Gordon and Reese came in through the front door.

"Okay, folks, nobody makes a move, nobody gets hurt. We are the Renegade Outlaws. We are going to make a quick withdrawal and be on our way." Riley pulled the knife out of the teller's hand and removed his hand from his mouth, muttering, "Open the vault."

As the teller opened the vault, all you could see was thousands upon thousands of US dollars and gold coins. While Gordon and Sissy filled up the saddlebags, Reese continuously looked outside to see if any trouble was coming. So far, none. Sissy and Gordon continued to fill up the bags, and the teller looked at Riley and at the door, then back at Riley and at his watch.

Riley caught on and said, "Why so jumpy, boy?"

The teller responded, "Looking at all this blood, I feel faint."

But Riley was no fool. He knew the teller kept looking at the door and the clock for a reason. He leaned over and asked him, "Who walks through that door at nine o'clock in the morning?"

"I don't know what you're talking about," responded the teller.

"If you want me to put a hole in your other hand, I can arrange that. Now I'm going to ask you again, who walks through that door at nine o'clock?"

The teller responded, "The US postal inspector."

Riley looked at the door, looked back at the teller, and said, "Now that wasn't so hard, was it?" He stuck his knife into the teller's stomach and said, "That's for lying the first time I asked you. I hate liars."

While Sissy and Gordon finished loading up the bags, Reese yelled, "Postal inspector!"

Reese grabbed the postal inspector and told him, "Don't make a move. We are just about done. Now we're going to finish our business, we're gonna walk out of here like nothing ever happened. Got it?"

The postal inspector, afraid, nodded.

Sissy, Gordon, Reese, and Riley, with their guns pointed at everyone, walked out the door without a sound. As the postal inspector looked over the desk, he saw the dead teller. The Renegade Outlaws slowly mounted their horses.

The postal inspector ran out of the bank, yelling, "Murderers! The teller was my son!"

As the postal inspector drew his gun, all four outlaws shot him. The gunfire caught the attention of some guys coming out of a saloon, and bullets began flying everywhere. The outlaws began riding and making their way toward the Mexican border while three other men rode behind them.

One of the guys yelled out, "Riley!" Apparently, he recognized Riley and the others from the wanted posters. These three other men were bounty hunters, and they were looking to collect. Shots were being fired by these three men.

All of a sudden, Gordon got hit in the back and fell off his horse. The other three stopped their horses and came to Gordon's aid.

During the shootout, Riley had Gordon covered and was able to hit one of the men right between the eyes, giving the outlaws the advantage. One of the bounty hunters apparently got up and shot Riley in the arm. Sissy, realizing they shot the love of her life, got on her horse and, like a wild woman, began yelling and shooting her two six-shooters in the direction of the last two bounty hunters, somehow hitting both of them in the chest. Sissy turned the horse around and got back to the others.

"You okay, darling?" Sissy asked Riley.

Riley responded, "Just a scratch." Sissy grabbed Riley and Gordon and pulled out her bowie knife, proceeding to take out both bullets out of her boys' arms.

"You know, we have a lot of money, and we ain't in no condition to fight right now. I say we pull up to those border patrol troopers and pay them some of this money we took from the bank."

"You want me to give those bastards some of the money I worked so hard to steal?" Riley paused. "Okay."

As the Renegade Outlaws pulled up to the border patrol officers, Reese said to the six of them, "I'm sure you know who we are. We are the Renegade Outlaws, and we are all worth $2,500 apiece. Now if you do the math, that's not very much to split between six men."

Sissy intruded, "But now if you fine gentlemen would just let us cross the border into Mexico, we just pulled a job in the bank of El Paso, and we are willing to pay each one of you gentlemen $5,000 apiece. What do you say?"

The officers looked at each other and took the bribe. All six officers were handed a bag full of American dollars and gold coins. As the Renegade Outlaws started making their way to the border, Riley turned around and said, "Oh, ah, by the way, those bags are still ours." All four outlaws drew their guns and shot the six border patrol officers dead. Reese jumped off his horse, grabbed all the bags, looked at Riley, and said, "Did they really think we were that easy? Ha ha!"

Riley responded, "Come on, guys. It's time to start our new lives as free men."

Sissy looked at Riley, and Riley responded, "And woman."

*****

The next morning, I took the rosary beads that Pedro made for me and went to pray in the convent. That morning, I decided to take a walk through the open land with my rosaries in hand, praying for all the dead souls in the Civil War. You know, the year is 1865; the war started in 1861. I couldn't believe, as I prayed, that this war had lasted so long.

Thinking about the Civil War got me to thinking about Captain Tuckett, and I would start thinking about his six-shooter, which he said would drive away evil spirits. It's been months since I shot a gun, and out of curiosity, I wanted to know if I could still shoot well. I walked over to the closet and pulled out the six-shooter. As I went to put the holster around my waist, the statue of Jesus Christ near the closet kept on staring at me. I knew that six-shooter and holster were not for shooting; it was a special gift given to Captain Tuckett by his father. I took the holster from around my waist and placed it back in the closet.

Later that day, I visited Mayor Fernandez and asked him if he would meet me behind the mission at around four o'clock. I told Mayor Fernandez to bring his rifle and guns.

"Are you in some kind of trouble, Padre?" he asked.

I told him, "No, it's just an itch I have that needs to be scratched."

*****

At four o'clock, we went far into the open land way behind the mission. As Mayor Fernandez brought the rifle and guns to me, I quickly began shooting at some bottles and cacti that I had laid out. At first, I was off. I mean, the last time I held a gun was months ago in the Civil War, but before you knew it, I was back to my sharp-shooting, quick-drawing self again. Mayor Fernandez was very impressed, and I must say, so was I.

Mayor Fernandez looked at me and said, "How did you learn to shoot like that?"

He knew about my Civil War background, but he didn't know that I was one of the US Army's top frontline soldiers.

"I still got it, Mayor."

He responded, "Yes, you still got it, Padre. You can go ahead and keep the guns for your target practice. I have three more at home just like them."

I thanked him, and off he went. That day, I stood out there shooting till the sun set. It was a lot more fun shooting bottles and cans than it was shooting human beings. I decided for fun to go out there every afternoon and practice after praying, just to be alone and for relaxation.

*****

A few days of practicing my shooting went by, and one morning, I went to the convent and prayed with the rosaries. After I was done, I went to my office, and there was Carmen waiting for me with a look of fear in her eyes.

"What happened?" I asked her, and she handed me the newspaper. My eyes opened up in shock when I saw the headline "RENEGADE OUTLAWS IN MEXICO." I read about the Federal Reserve Bank of El Paso being robbed. I read about the young teller and postal inspector being killed, the three dead bounty hunters, and the six dead border patrol officers.

I always knew it. I read all about their robberies and knew they were making their way to Mexico, but I didn't want to accept it. My worst enemy, the murderer of my best friend, the man who shot out my eye, living in the same place I'm living in. My heart pounded with fear, my palms once again were full of sweat. I said nothing to Carmen. I just grabbed my rosaries and ran to the church to pray.

"Please, Lord," I prayed, "keep these outlaws as far away from Saragosa as possible. I dedicated my life to you and asked for nothing in return. Now I'm asking—no, I am begging—please keep Riley and his gang as far away from Saragosa as possible. Amen."

When I left the church, Pedro saw that I was in a state of shock and tried to console me.

"Padre, are you okay?"

"Yes, Pedro, I am okay, just a little tired."

Pedro responded, "Come on, Padre, I'll walk you to the convent." As Pedro grabbed my hand and began walking me over to the convent, he began to sing the song of the "Star-Spangled Banner," and for the first time, hearing him sing did nothing for me.

I told Pedro to get back to the other children in the mission and lock all doors—something I never had to worry about because I always felt safe with the mission, church, and school that God gave me.

*****

Riley and Sissy were drinking whiskey at a local saloon when Reese and Gordon came crashing through the doors, each with a paper in hand.

"Riley," Gordon said, "It's gonna be harder to live a straight life in Mexico than we thought."

Riley responded, "What the hell you talking about?"

Gordon handed him the paper and said, "We are known all throughout Mexico."

Reese added, "There ain't no decent people out here in Mexico that are gonna be willing to deal with us."

"Hey!" Riley yelled. "I said once we got to Mexico, we would have enough money between the four of us to live a fair and decent life. All the shooting and bloodshed is now over. This is the beginning of a new life for all of us. We are all gonna march up to the authorities, buy us some land the honest way, own a business the honest way, and get old, fat, and happy the honest way. We've come too far to let a small thing like this stand in the way of each one of us from living an honest life. Everything will be done fairly, and we'll all be all right. I promise."

Sissy looked at Riley as he watched Reese and Gordon leave and said to him, "How much of that was true?"

Riley responded, "All of it, and if these Mexican greasers don't want to sell us no land, then I guess we'll just have to do what we do best and take whatever we want." Sissy wanted to have a large piece of land and a nice big house to call her own, and that's exactly what Riley intended on giving her.

*****

All four went the next morning to visit some landowners who were looking to sell, but every single landowner recognized all the outlaws and didn't want to do business. All the businessmen made up phony excuses to get rid of the four outlaws in a hurry.

"You see!" Gordon yelled, "None of these people are going to give us a break, Riley. They know about us. They've read about us in the papers. No one is going to want to do business with a bunch of murdering, stealing outlaws on the run."

Riley responded, "We keep on heading south and keep on trying. Let's not give up, okay, guys? We've never given up before, and we ain't about to start now."

"Riley," Sissy responded, "the guys are right."

Riley interrupted, "I don't care! We, and especially I, did not come this far to let a small thing like this stop me. Now, tomorrow, we are going to meet with two more landowners, and if they don't give us what we want, we'll just have to take it."

Sissy spoke, "Take it? We can't just take it. We can't rob or steal or kill anymore, baby. This is it. We can't cross the border back to the States. We're wanted there. And we can't go around stealing, robbing, and killing, because then the Mexican government would want us too."

Riley, enraged, responded, "I don't care!"

Gordon and Reese agreed. "You're right, Riley. Tomorrow, we bring all our cash and gold coins and try to do business. If they don't cooperate, then we'll force our way into a happy life."

Sissy smiled but was at a loss for words.

*****

The next day, the four outlaws brought all their saddlebags full of money and gold coins with them to all of their appointments and again were turned down. Riley, enraged, told the rest of the guys, "I need a drink!"

As the four went to drink at a local saloon, Riley looked at Gordon and said, "You know what, Gordy? I've always wanted to own a bar. Hey, bartender, who owns this place?"

It was late, and the four were the only ones in the saloon. "I do," responded the bartender.

"Tell you what, pal, here's five thousand in cash and gold coins. Hand over the ownership papers."

"Well, you see, señor—"

Before the bartender could say another word, Riley shot him right in the stomach. "Looks like I'm the new owner of the General Saloon."

Riley and Sissy went upstairs, and Gordon and Reese hopped on their horses and rode off into the night. The next morning, Reese and Gordon informed Sissy and Riley that they had held up two hotels and wiped out the owners. Now Riley owned the saloon, and Gordon and Reese each owned a hotel.

"Now it's time to look for some land!" Riley yelled.

*****

The four outlaws rode further south. They all went to their newly acquired businesses and introduced themselves as the new bosses. They didn't care about living close to their businesses. They just cared about how much money was coming in every week. As they continued to ride, they rode up into the small town of Saragosa.

Sissy jumped off her horse and asked a little girl if there was any open land in Saragosa. The little girl said no, and the last piece of big land was already taken up when they built the church. Sissy thanked the girl and told Riley.

The four Renegade Outlaws rode up to Mayor Fernandez's office. Mayor Fernandez quickly recognized all four and went for his gun. All four drew a lot quicker but didn't shoot. Riley spoke, "Now why so jumpy, Mayor? We just want to talk. Now it appears that a big chunk of land was bought a few months ago here in Saragosa. Now who bought all that land?"

The mayor responded, "Father Pinekin. He opened up the first church, mission, and school for the people of Saragosa."

"Well, isn't that nice?" Riley responded, not remembering the name Pinekin. "Now, Mayor, you run over there and tell those kind folks that as of today, the church, mission, and school is closed forever."

The mayor, in panic, said, "I cannot do that."

Riley responded, "Okay then. I tried to do it the nice way. Here's the deal, mayor: since you don't want to do it the easy way, we'll just have to do it the hard way." All four outlaws gunned Mayor Fernandez down and rode off to the church. Gordon pulled out some whiskey bottles, and the outlaws began to first burn down the school, then proceeded to burn the mission.

*****

The yells and screams of little children caught my attention as I was praying with my rosaries in the church. As I ran out, I could see children from the mission screaming in fear. As I looked further, I could even see some children in flames.

"Stop!" I yelled. "Stop!" but these four people would not. As I ran to the well to try and stop the flames, I realized that the four outlaws had made their way to the church and were proceeding to burn it down. I begged and pleaded as a man of God, but the outlaws would not stop. All of a sudden, I saw him.

"Riley!" I yelled as I got down on my knees.

Riley turned to me and said, "Padre, do I know you?" As Riley looked closer, he recognized who I was.

"Pinekin! Well, what a small world. Damn, I thought I killed you back in the war. Now I see all I did was shoot your eye off!"

"Please, Riley," I begged, hunched over a large rock, "there are innocent children in there. One of them made these four rosary beads for me."

Riley responded, "Well, ain't that nice? But I'm sorry, Padre. I promised Sissy a big home, and this is the only way I can do it."

As I looked up, I heard Carmen screaming. As I ran to go to her aid, Riley yelled, "Hey, Padre, this time I won't miss!" and shot me down. I grabbed my four rosaries, and out I went. Never would I have thought this would happen to me.

*****

As I got up the next morning off the ground, it appeared that Riley shot me in the shoulder and not the heart. I paused and looked around me. Innocent victims were dead, my school burned to the ground, and my mission was gone. When I walked over to the church, I realized that the cross that was on top of my church was now behind it. As I walked over, tears came to my eyes and a hurtful pain came to my heart.

Apparently, one of the outlaws raped Carmen, killed her, and hung her naked on my cross. As I hugged Carmen and proceeded to cry, I heard Pedro calling me. I rushed over to him so that he wouldn't see Carmen.

That day, Pedro went over to Mayor Fernandez's house to have supper with Mayor Fernandez and his wife. He told me that Mayor Fernandez never made it home that night and that he and Mrs. Fernandez found the mayor dead in his office. I hugged them both and told them to go back home. As they left, I proceeded to dig a grave for Carmen and the others.

After I was done, I went to what was left of the church and saw the statue of Jesus Christ by the closet.

"Why?" I yelled. "Tell me, Lord, why? I made a deal with you. I told you if I survived the Civil War, I would dedicate my life to you. Why are you putting me through this pain and agony? What, Lord, would make these evil spirits go away for good?"

I threw a rock at the statue, knocking it over and opening up the closet. There was my answer: the black box that Captain Tuckett gave me. I opened it with tears in my eyes and realized what I now needed to do. I took off my cassock, strapped on the holster, put the six-shooter in the holster, and loaded up on the bullets that Mayor Fernandez gave me.

As I brought my horse to the burned-down church with my six-shooter by my side and my rifle in the saddle holster, I took my hat off, got on my knees, put the four rosaries around my holster, and proceeded to say what would be my last prayer as a priest. "God, forgive me for the evil I am about to do, but there is no other way to drive out these evil spirits."

I got on my horse and took my white collar off from around my neck, placing it on the broken statue. Off I rode into the sunset on what would be a mission of mercy.

As I rode north past Saragosa, I heard Pedro call me. "Padre, where are you going?"

I responded, "I must go now, niño, but before anything, come with me." I put Pedro behind me and rode off to Mayor Fernandez's house. I spoke to Mrs. Fernandez about looking after Pedro. Mayor and Mrs. Fernandez never had any kids of their own, and I thought it would be a good idea for them both to stay together.

"Will I ever see you again, Padre?"

I responded, "I don't know, niño. We'll just leave it in the Lord's hands."

*****

As I rode north, I couldn't get these four outlaws out of my mind and what they did to me. I pulled up to a saloon for some water when I realized the saloon was empty in the middle of the afternoon.

"Bartender, toss me some water." The bartender gave me the water. "Why is business so dead so early?"

The bartender spoke, "Those outlaws came in and scared everyone."

"Where are they?" I asked.

"No, señor, this was two days ago."

I replied, "What did they look like?"

"Three men and one little lady. They said they were going to make all the business and land theirs."

"Okay," I replied. "You tell these outlaws when you see them that *El Padre* is looking for them, you got that?"

The bartender swallowed nervously and nodded. Since I knew I wasn't that far from the outlaws, I decided to stay at a nearby hotel. Old habits are hard to break. As I went down to the hotel lobby to read the newspaper, I realized that the headlines read that the mayor of Saragosa was murdered by unknown people. At that point in time, I decided to take a ride to the Mexican governor's house. Governor Peña had visited my church in Saragosa many times and was a good friend of Mayor Fernandez.

After I rode up to the house, Governor Peña greeted me outside and took me in.

"How have you been, Father Pinekin?"

I responded, "Don't call me that. I'm no longer a priest, Governor. I know who the outlaws who killed Mayor Fernandez are."

"Who are they?" Governor Peña asked anxiously.

"They are the same outlaws who burned down my mission and church and raped and killed my best friend Carmen. Mayor

Fernandez was a good man, and he didn't deserve to die. And these four outlaws are gonna get what's coming to them. They are also the four outlaws wanted by the US government."

"Well, now they are wanted by the Mexican government!" Governor Peña responded.

I rudely replied, "No! How much would you ask for all four outlaws, dead or alive?"

Governor Peña held up five fingers and responded, "Five thousand a head. I'll have the press print it, and they'll be gone quickly."

I interrupted, "It's not that simple, Governor. The three men are all trained professional soldiers who fought in the Civil War back home, and the one lady is probably crazier than all three. Riley is the one who shot my eye off in the Civil War. They were wanted men back in the States, and nobody could catch them, so they made their way to Mexico. Now they are bullying their way into owning businesses and taking over innocent people's land. If you print a wanted poster or story about them being wanted in the papers, they will hide so well that they would never be found. So I say, Governor, five grand apiece is good for me. I have a personal score to settle with them. Don't say or print anything. Let them go on living like nothing is wrong, and that way I can strike at them one by one."

Governor Peña responded, "You mean you want to hunt these men for a bounty, Father Pinekin?"

"Yes, let's just call this our personal deal, and I told you, I am no longer a priest."

As I left and got on my horse, I could hear Governor Peña saying, "You got it, Padre. Give them hell, and I will reward you."

Off I rode into the night to look for my destiny. As I rode up to the hotel, I could not stop thinking of what I was doing. I grabbed my holster and thought about Captain Tuckett. I always felt that he was wrong, but at the same time, he was right. No matter how much I prayed and begged God to keep these outlaws away from me, they just wouldn't go away. After my church and mission were burned to the ground and Carmen was killed, Captain Tuckett's way seemed the only way to get rid of those evil souls forever.

As I looked at myself in the mirror, I didn't even appear to be the same man. All of a sudden, I heard the yell of a woman outside.

"What's the matter, señorita?"

She responded, "There's a man in the saloon going crazy."

I grabbed her and told her to stay in the hotel lobby. As I walked over to the saloon, I could hear one man yelling. As I entered, there was Reese. He was beating up the bartender with his back toward me.

"What the hell do you mean El Padre was looking for me? Who the hell is this Padre anyway, and what does he want with me?"

I responded, "I am El Padre, and I want your ass dead!" Reese went for his gun, but I drew quicker and managed to shoot him in the chest.

As I walked over to him, I could see that he was still alive.

"Where are the others?" Reese didn't respond, so I asked again, "Where are the others?"

Reese looked up at me and said, "Go to hell, priest!"

I responded, "No, you first," and shot him dead on the saloon floor. I reached back behind my holster, pulled out my red rosary, and stuck it in his mouth.

I grabbed his dead body, mounted it on my horse, and proceeded to tell the townspeople, "This is one of the Renegade Outlaws. If any of you see a woman named Sissy, a man named Gordon, or a man named Riley, you tell them El Padre killed one of their best friends, and I am coming back for the rest of them!"

A slow hush came over the crowd, then cheers erupted. As I rode off to Governor Peña's house to collect the unknown bounty, I could say that this was the first time since the Civil War that I killed a man, and I must admit, deep down inside that this was only the beginning, and it would only get worse. I collected my bounty and rode off. I didn't want to carry that much money on me, so I went straight to a local bank in town to deposit the five grand.

*****

Riley, Sissy, and Gordon went to the bar for a drink around nine. "Where the hell is Reese? That son of a bitch is always late."

After two hours passed, they realized Reese wasn't going to show up. "Reese never misses our get-togethers."

A young man passing by overheard Riley and said, "You looking for Reese, señor? Reese is dead."

Riley grabbed the young man and put him on the floor. "What do you mean dead? How? When?"

The young man responded, "Early yesterday, in the saloon."

Riley, in anger, responded, "Who did it? Who killed Reese?"

The young man told him, "I don't know him. He was a stranger in this town. He was tall, wore black clothes, had a patch over his eye, and said his name was El Padre.

Riley let the guy go and told Sissy and Gordon, "*El Padre* is Spanish for 'the priest.' I only know one priest with a patch over his eye. Pinekin is after us."

Gordon said, "Pinekin? We killed Pinekin when we took over his land, Riley."

Riley responded, "You know, Gord, back home in the war, I shot his eye off. I thought he was dead then. Then, I burned everything he owned and shot him in front of his burning church, and again, I thought he was dead. It's almost like he's some kind of angel on a mercy mission that won't die. And now he's come back and killed one of my own."

Riley looked at Sissy and said, "Sissy, we drove a priest out of his church, and he's coming after us to kill us, so be alert."

Gordon looked at Riley, confused, and said, "Hey, Riley, why are you so worried about some sissy priest boy? What's the difference between him and all the other guys we've killed?"

Riley responded, "He's not an ordinary sissy priest. Back in the war, he was those bluecoat bastards' top frontline soldier. As you can see, he ain't an easy man to kill, and he's hungry after our heads, which makes him that much more dangerous. We find him. We strike first. I don't care this time—we make sure he's dead."

*****

The following day, I sat in Peña's office and told him that with an old horse as my companion, it was hard to put a dead corpse and ride. Not only that, but I didn't want to lead a trail between me and the governor. So I told him after every hit, I would send him a telegram so he could get one of his men to bury the body.

At the hotel where I was staying, I would always read the *World News* newspaper. When I came to a halt, there was an ad for the Lonestar Hotel, and at the bottom, it said for more info, speak to the owner, Mr. Gordon. I quickly jumped on my horse and headed for the Lonestar Hotel.

As I rode up to the hotel, a man in front began to open fire. It appeared that Gordon recognized me on sight. With bullets flying everywhere, no one got the upper hand. Next thing I knew, bullets were coming at me from the right. As I got a better look, I realized that a tall man and a short woman were shooting at me. It was Riley and Sissy. It then hit me that I was set up, so the only thing I could do, being outnumbered three to one, was make my way to my horse and have them follow me. As I hopped on my horse, I could hear the footsteps running after me.

BANG, BANG, BANG! was all I heard as I rode off into the woods. I looked back and saw all three after me. I quickly jumped off my horse and made my way behind some bushes. From where I was, I could see all three clearly. I got up and began shooting at them. I hit Gordon in the shoulder, and he went down and hid in the bushes. Riley was my main target. As I carefully reloaded my six-shooter, I quickly began getting flashbacks of the Civil War—rebels shooting at me, reloading my gun, hiding in the bushes… Then all of a sudden, I came back to reality, and there was Riley, looking for me with his back to me.

I stood up and yelled at him, "TURN AROUND, RILEY!" he quickly turned and pointed his gun at me. As I saw him draw his gun in my direction, I fired first.

Out of nowhere, I heard a yell, "No!" Sissy jumped in front of the bullet and got shot in the chest. Riley grabbed Sissy, and Gordon began shooting at me again. As I shot back at Gordon, I could hear Riley crying and begging Sissy not to die. As I hid behind a rock, I heard Gordon yell at Riley, "There's a hospital back in town, Riley. Go now."

Riley, crying and holding onto his number one love, looked at Gordon and shook his head. Gordon yelled, "Go, Riley! Go save Sissy."

As Riley mounted Sissy on his horse, I got up and began shooting at Riley, but I couldn't hit him. I was too far out of range. As I ran behind Riley, Gordon came out of nowhere, and—*BANG!*— I was able to shoot him in the chest. As I made my way toward him, I could see the blood coming out of his mouth. I looked down at Gordon, and he said to me, "My own blood tastes as good as your greasy girlfriend."

When he told me that, I realized he was the one who raped and killed Carmen. Without thinking twice about it, I shot him right between the eyes. I reached back behind my holster, pulled out my white rosary, and stuck it in his mouth. I whistled, and my horse came. I knew where I was going. Riley loved Sissy and would no doubt try to have her saved, so I made my way to the hospital.

*****

Riley, begging Sissy to hold on, was crying and saw Sissy losing a lot of blood. Sissy looked at Riley and said, "I love you, baby. Too bad we couldn't get married in time." Riley grabbed one of the doctors and said, "Find me a priest, fast." The doctor ran down the hall, grabbed a priest, and brought him over. Riley looked at the priest and said, "Marry us as soon as possible."

The priest responded, "I will perform the ceremony, but you must keep the guns outside. I will not perform a wedding with evil guns present."

Riley, desperate to grant Sissy's last wish, grabbed his guns and put them outside. He came back, and the priest proceeded, "Do you, Steve Edward Riley, take Sissy Sason as your lawfully wedded wife?"

Riley responded, "I do."

"Do you, Sissy Sason, take Steve Edward Riley as your lawfully wedded husband?"

Sissy, gasping for air, responded, "I do."

The priest continued, "If there is anyone who feels that these two should not be together in holy matrimony, let them speak now or forever hold their peace."

All of a sudden, a cold voice from nowhere said, "I object." Riley, realizing who it was, grabbed the priest and put his bowie knife to the man's neck.

Pinekin, with his gun drawn in the direction of Riley, stared coldly into Riley's eyes. "How dare you? How dare you interrupt this sacred moment of peace?"

Pinekin responded, "'Sacred'? 'Peace'? Do you even know what those two words you just said mean? *Peace*—to live your life with no hardship, no pain, no agony, and no hate. *Sacred*—to hold something near and dear to your heart with love. You have no right to even mention those two words, Riley."

Riley, looking at Sissy, saw her close her eyes slowly and stop breathing. Riley yelled, "No!"

Pinekin, trying to get a clear shot at Riley, moved closer.

Riley looked at Pinekin and said, "Don't move, Pinekin, or I'll do the priest!"

Pinekin responded, "Go ahead. I don't care. Take him out. Don't you realize the moment you kill him, I kill you? Not only that, but the sight of a white collar makes me want to puke. You see, Riley, I used to care. I used to love, but when you burned down my church and killed my friends and family, you took away from me all that I cared for and loved. You remember Captain Tuckett? This right here is his six-shooter, and with his very own gun, I will kill you!"

Riley, surprised at what he was hearing, responded, "You want to kill me, Pinekin? I'll give you the opportunity."

Riley, walking backward, still holding on to the priest, looked over one last time at Sissy and told Pinekin, "Meet me in two hours at your old church in Saragosa." Riley threw his bowie knife at Pinekin as ran out, getting his guns, and hopped on his horse. By the time Pinekin ran outside, Riley was a big cloud of dust, but Pinekin knew he now had a date with destiny.

Pinekin went back into the hospital and walked right into the room where Sissy lay dead. The priest looked at Pinekin and said, "Señor, you must go before the sheriff arrives." Pinekin looked at Sissy with cold eyes, reached behind his holster, pulled out his blue rosary, and stuck it in Sissy's mouth.

*****

As I rode off to the hotel where I was staying, I realized that this was the first time since my church was burned that I returned to Saragosa. I quietly rode to the hotel and realized that I had to tell Governor Peña about the other two outlaws. I rode to the postal service and quickly sent him a telegram. I couldn't stop thinking about Saragosa and how much I didn't want to go back there, but I had no choice. If I wanted to rid the world and myself of Riley, I had to go. I took one last look at myself in the mirror, put on my black hat, reloaded my holster and my six-shooter, and off I went to Saragosa.

As I mounted my horse and rode to Saragosa, I kept getting flashbacks of that son of a bitch Riley and his gang burning down my church. All of a sudden, I stopped and saw the sign that said, "WELCOME TO SARAGOSA"—the same sign I saw a few months ago when I rode into Saragosa to start my new life. Now I was riding into the same small Mexican town to reach my destiny.

As I slowly rode past the bushes and trees, I passed by Mayor Fernandez's house quietly so no one could see or hear me. As I continued riding, I could hear a voice from afar yelling at me. "Padre, Padre!" As I turned around, I saw Pedro riding a small mule toward me. He jumped off his mule and ran toward me. I quickly jumped off my horse and hugged him.

"Where have you been, Padre? We've missed you!"

I responded, "I have been out sending evil spirits to their destiny, niño. You must do me a favor, Pedro. You must not let anyone know that I am back in Saragosa. Understand?"

Pedro, confused, replied, "But, Padre—?"

I quickly interrupted, "Don't call me that anymore, niño. I am no longer a priest. Now get back on your mule and ride back home, niño."

"But, Padre—"

I responded angrily, "No buts, niño. Go home, and do not call me that."

As Pedro turned and walked toward his mule, I could hear him weeping. I quickly turned my horse around, grabbed my last blue-and-yellow rosary, and headed toward my old church. As I rode, I could see from afar the ashes of what was once my church. In front stood Riley. I paused for a second, stared at Riley, then proceeded to ride closer.

"Glad you can make it, Pinekin. See, here was where I was gonna live the rest of my life with my beautiful Sissy and our kids, and you took all that away."

I responded, "You know, Riley, you killed Captain Tuckett, and I learned to deal with that. You shot my eye off, and I learned to deal with that. But then you came to Saragosa, burned down everything that I held so near and dear to my heart, and left my family including my best friend raped and murdered. That I couldn't deal with. Riley, you shot me and left me for dead a couple of times. But I never died. You know why? Because I am an angel of mercy sent here to rid the world of evil people like you."

*****

Riley yells, "ENOUGH!"

Pinekin responds, "That's right. Enough!"

Both men circled each other, looking for a good spot for the draw. Riley studied the sun and walked around, keeping the sun behind his back like a veteran gunfighter. Pinekin didn't care about anything, staying right where he was.

"I'm gonna kill you, Pinekin. This time, I guarantee, I won't miss."

Pinekin, in his drawing stance, didn't respond.

Both men, with hate in their heart and vengeance running through their veins, silently and coldly stared at each other. The seconds went like hours, neither man flinching—until finally, the draw!

Gunshots went off—one from each man, responding in turn. Riley. Pinekin. Riley. Pinekin. Riley. Pinekin…

Suddenly, "Aghhh!" Riley yelled in pain, holding his chest as he slowly sank to the floor.

Pinekin walked toward the fallen Riley, taking his time. Riley looked up at Pinekin with fear, and Pinekin looked down at Riley. "That was for Captain Tuckett."

He shot Riley again. "That was for Carmen."

He shot Riley a third time. "That was for all the children in my mission you left dead or homeless."

Pinekin slowly loaded more bullets into his six-shooter. *BANG, BANG, BANG, BANG, BANG, BANG!* "That was for me."

And Riley was dead.

Pinekin spun his gun and put it in his holster. He pulled out his blue-and-yellow rosary and stuck it in what was left of Riley's mouth.

*****

As I mounted my horse and rode almost out of the town, I could hear Pedro yelling at me once again, "Padre!" But this time, he was with Mrs. Fernandez. I got off my horse, emotionally hugged them both, and told them, "You guys will never see me again, but I can guarantee that Saragosa will again have a school, a church, and a mission, I promise. Goodbye, Mrs. Fernandez."

I slowly kneeled down, hugged Pedro, and said, "Adios, niño."

Pedro looked at me with tears in his eyes and said, "Adios, Padre."

As I mounted my horse and headed out of Saragosa, I heard Pedro call out, "Padre! Padre! We love you, Padre! You will never be forgotten! Adios!"

*****

The next day, I left the hotel, arriving later at Governor Peña's house.

"The rest of the Renegade Outlaws have been killed. I am here to collect my secret bounty."

Governor Peña went into his safe and handed me fifteen thousand along with the other five thousand I already had when Governor Peña paid me for killing Reese first.

I laid out all twenty thousand on his desk and grabbed just five thousand, telling Governor Peña, "This here is my five thousand for taking Riley. The rest of the fifteen thousand, you take to Saragosa. Rebuild the people there a new church, school, and mission."

Governor Peña looked at me and said, "You have my word, señor, the people of Saragosa will definitely have all that you have requested."

I grabbed my five thousand and grabbed Peña's *World News* newspaper from his desk. As I mounted my horse, I looked at the newspaper and read the headline: "Robert E. Lee Surrenders His Southern Army."

It was May 9. The Civil War had ended, and the Northern US Army had won. But in reality, we all lost more than we had gained.

The End

www.ingramcontent.com/pod-product-compliance
Lightning Source LLC
Chambersburg PA
CBHW022038150726
47990CB00004B/1519